Phantom
Gardener

backpack MYSTERIES

9701

3

a backpack mystery

Phantom Gardener

Mary Carpenter Reid

BETHANY HOUSE PUBLISHERS
MINNEAPOLIS, MINNESOTA 55438

Phantom Gardener
Copyright © 1997
Mary Carpenter Reid

Cover and story illustrations by Paul Turnbaugh

Published by Bethany House Publishers
A Ministry of Bethany Fellowship, Inc.
11300 Hampshire Avenue South
Minneapolis, Minnesota 55438

Printed in the United States of America.

Library of Congress Cataloging-in-Publication Data

Reid, Mary.
    Phantom gardener / by Mary Carpenter Reid.
       p. cm. — (A Backpack mystery ; 3)
    Summary: Steff and her younger sister Paulie are staying at a retirement community with their grandmother, an avid gardener, when they hear stories about a phantom gardener who works at night and a thief who is stealing plants.
ISBN 1–55661–717–8
    [1. Gardening—Fiction. 2. Grandmothers—Fiction. 3. Christian life—Fiction. 4. Mystery and detective stories.] I. Title. II. Series: Reid, Mary. Backpack mystery ; 3.
PZ7.R2727Ph   1996
[Fic]—dc21   97–4649
                                             CIP
                                           AC

To Holly—
a special person in my family.

MARY CARPENTER REID loves to visit places just like the places Steff and Paulie visit. Does she stay with peculiar relatives? That's her secret!

She will tell you her family is wonderful. She likes reading and writing children's books. She like colors and computers. She especially likes getting letters from her readers.

She can't organize things as well as Steff does, but she makes lots of lists.

Two cats—a calico and a tiger cat—live at her house in California. *They* are very peculiar!

contents

Honor your father and your mother.

Exodus 20:12

Lily pad park

Steff Larson raced along the sidewalk. She tried to keep up with her mother's car.

But the car moved far ahead on the winding street. It grew smaller and smaller in the evening light.

Steff couldn't run any longer. She held her side with one hand and waved with the other.

The car stopped to let a golf cart cross the street. Her mother's arm reached out the window and returned Steff's wave.

Steff waved harder.

The car drove out of sight. It was headed toward the front gate of Lily Pad Park. The iron gate would swing open. Her mother would drive out. The gate would clang shut.

Steff turned back to Uncle Joe's house. She and Paulie had been left with relatives again.

Paulie stood on the curb, still waving.

Steff didn't like to see her younger sister looking so alone. "Hey, Paulie, want to skip rope? I brought my rope."

Paulie shook her head. She said, "I saw tears on Mom's cheeks."

Steff sighed. She knew her mother was crying as she drove away. She knew her parents had started the family business because they had to—when her father had been laid off from his job. But sometimes it was hard for Steff to remember that all these trips her parents made were for the business—not for fun.

Especially this time when Steff wanted to go with them.

Especially here in this community for older people. She and Paulie were *younger* people. A lot younger. The sign by the gate said Lily Pad

Park was a retirement golf community for ACTIVE seniors.

Uncle Joe Quigg had retired six months ago. Then he and his mother moved here.

Mother Quigg was 80 years old. She reminded Steff of the front lawn of the new house—tiny, with a short haircut.

She called, "Girls, come see the backyard."

Mother Quigg wore a hat with a floppy brim. A bright pink scarf was tied around the hat and hung down behind. Fresh daisies were tucked in her belt and pinned on her blouse. More daisies flapped on the tops of her shoes as she walked.

"Oooh," said Paulie. "Look at the flowers. This is the prettiest backyard in the world."

"Mother takes care of the back," said Uncle Joe. "The Lily Pad Park Homeowners Group has a grounds crew. They do all the other gardening in the community. We don't even mow our front lawn."

Mother Quigg said, "Here is one of my favorite flowers—larkspur."

Uncle Joe tossed a golf ball from one hand

to the other. "This retirement home is perfect for Mother and me. I play golf every day except Sunday. We go to church on Sunday."

Steff asked, "Do children live at Lily Pad Park?"

Uncle Joe ran a hand through his gray hair. "No—except for that boy in the corner house. But he's usually away at school. His parents travel a lot. No one is there now."

In the garage, Uncle Joe pointed to two golf carts. One was pink. It had a pink top to shade the driver. A pink flag flew above the pink top.

"I bought Mother her own golf cart. Pretty fancy—huh, Mother?"

He didn't wait for her to answer. "I hired someone to do the housework. Mother has plenty of time to play golf."

After they had seen the golf carts, they went inside.

Uncle Joe sat down to read a golfing magazine.

Mother Quigg showed the girls their room and said she was going to bed.

It was only eight o'clock.

Steff guessed Mother Quigg must be tired. After all, she was 80 years old.

Steff and Paulie went to bed, too.

Steff kept waking up. A mini-blind covered the bedroom window. Light came through.

Her backpack hung from a chair.

She tried to pretend she was seeing her backpack on a chair in her bedroom at home.

She tried to pretend she was lying in her bed at home.

She couldn't. She pulled the sheet over her face.

Then she heard a strange noise. *SCR-A-A-P-E!*

She huddled under the sheet. Maybe—just maybe—Paulie had made the strange noise.

No. Paulie lay sleeping on the other half of the trundle bed.

More noises sounded. *GROAN—CREAK—CREAK—CLUNK!*

Their bedroom was at the front of the house. Steff tiptoed to the window. She peeked through the mini-blind.

Lily Pad Park was brightly lit with

streetlights. Lamps glowed on brick posts in front of each house. Lights shone on trees.

Steff saw something odd.

"Paulie," Steff called. "Wake up! Get your clothes on. We are going outside."

NOISE AT THE EMPTY HOUSE

Paulie stumbled to the closet. "I can't find a shirt to match these pants."

Steff hissed, "Nothing has to match! Just hurry!"

A few minutes later, the girls slipped out the kitchen door. They stood on the driveway beside the house.

Steff pointed to a wilted daisy on the sidewalk. "Mother Quigg went that way."

"Mother Quigg is in bed." Paulie bent down and tied her shoes.

"No, she isn't. I saw her from the bedroom window. She drove away in her pink golf cart."

"Right, Steff. Like people play golf in the middle of the night."

Steff grabbed her sister's hand. "Let's find her. She might be in trouble or something. Besides, I'm not sleepy. We went to bed too early."

Paulie said, "I don't think we should go anyplace."

"Mom told us Lily Pad Park is a safe community. The guard at the gate lets in only people who should come in."

"If it is such a safe place, then Mother Quigg is safe. I think you just want to go exploring."

"Maybe. But I also want to know why Mother Quigg is driving her golf cart at night. Don't you?"

"I guess so."

Paulie followed Steff.

The many outdoor lights made it easy for the girls to see.

Across from Uncle Joe's house were large grassy areas. Flowers and trees dotted the open spaces. Trails for golf carts crisscrossed everywhere.

They were still on Uncle Joe's street when Steff pulled Paulie off the sidewalk. "Look over there! That could be a golf cart behind those trees."

Just then, the light coming from a lamp on a brick post behind them seemed to flicker.

Steff whirled.

Something—or someone—had darted between them and the lamp. They heard the sound of a door closing—a door on the corner house.

"Steff," Paulie whispered. "Didn't Uncle Joe say no one was there?"

"Y-yes!" Steff stammered.

"Let's get out of here!" Paulie squealed.

They raced back to the Quigg house.

3

a gardener that no one sees

The next morning, Steff and Paulie found a woman in the kitchen. She fixed breakfast and talked at the same time.

"I'm Gladys. Mr. Quigg is playing golf. He eats breakfast—and lunch—at the clubhouse."

Gladys set pancakes on the table. She kept talking. "Mother Quigg gets up late. Takes a nap every afternoon."

She poured orange juice.

"I leave at three o'clock. Mother Quigg

always fixes dinner for her and Mr. Quigg." She frowned. "Whether he eats it or not is another story."

The girls joined hands and bowed their heads. Gladys stopped talking while they said grace.

Steff asked her, "Do you know anything about the family in the corner house?"

"Oh, no. I never poke my nose into other people's business," Gladys said. "There is one boy. He goes to boarding school, the kind where the kids live there. The parents left yesterday morning. Later, a cab came to take the boy to school."

Paulie exclaimed, "But we heard—"

Steff's fist shot under the table and smacked Paulie's leg. Paulie tried to hit Steff's leg.

Steff grabbed Paulie's hand and held on.

She asked Gladys politely, "Does Lily Pad Park have lily pads?"

"Certainly. At the lake."

"When Mom drove us in, we saw flowers everywhere."

"Almost any flower can grow here. But

20

don't ever pick one." Gladys shook her finger. "The Homeowners Group will get you."

Paulie jerked her hand free. "Get you?"

Gladys said, "People here can do anything they want in their backyards. But the grounds crew takes care of the rest—the front yards and every other inch of the park."

"What could the Homeowners Group do to you?" Steff asked.

"I don't know. I just hear it's better to follow the rules." Gladys chuckled. "Of course, people say the Phantom Gardener doesn't follow the rules."

Steff nearly spilled her orange juice. "Phantom Gardener? A gardener that no one sees?"

Gladys nodded. "People say somebody planted red geraniums by the lake. Planted them in the shape of a cross. The grounds crew didn't plant those geraniums."

"Who did?" asked Paulie.

"No one knows. Just like no one knows how four bushes near the tennis courts suddenly changed to look like a mother rabbit and three baby rabbits."

"Rabbits?" Paulie giggled.

Gladys nodded. "Somebody trimmed the bushes in the shape of rabbits. The grounds crew didn't do that either."

Steff cut her pancake to look like a rabbit. Except it had three ears.

Paulie reached with her fork and stabbed one ear. She laughed and popped it into her mouth.

Gladys said, "Mr. Kemper did not think the rabbits were one bit funny. He is in charge of the Homeowners Group. Mother Quigg says that man is as prickly as a cactus."

Later that morning, Mother Quigg told the girls, "Let's take a ride around the park."

She put on her hat with the floppy brim. The pink scarf hung down her back. She wore a white carnation pinned to her shirt.

She pinned red carnations on the girls.

They found dirt on the pink golf cart. Everything else in the garage was clean.

Mother Quigg drove them over winding streets and golf cart trails.

They passed the grounds crew. They were

trimming bushes. Tools filled the back of the pickup truck. A closed truck that looked like a delivery truck was parked nearby.

Mother Quigg stopped her cart by the gate.

The guard leaned out the window of his guard house.

He told Mother Quigg, "The flowers near the flagpole look prettier this year than ever before."

Mother Quigg seemed pleased.

They drove on.

A closed truck, like the other truck, stopped to let their cart cross the street.

The driver frowned. He kept looking in the side mirror. Steff had never seen such big, bushy eyebrows.

Mother Quigg knew the names of all the plants. She even knew what kind of grass grew on the golf course.

"I like golf courses," she said. "But I don't care for golf. I told Joe that before we moved here."

"You have this pretty pink golf cart, though," said Paulie.

"Oh, I use it," Mother Quigg said. "I certainly do use it."

After lunch, Mother Quigg added another white carnation to her shirt. She put another red one on each girl. Then she went to take a nap.

After her nap, she fixed chicken and rice for dinner.

Uncle Joe did not come home until after dinner.

Mother Quigg told him, "I thought you were coming home for dinner."

He clapped a hand to his head. "Sorry. I got to talking golf and forgot. I ate at the clubhouse."

He showed the girls his golf trophies. They filled a whole wall.

Mother Quigg told the girls, "Don't stay up too late and don't forget to telephone your parents." She went to her room. It was eight o'clock.

Uncle Joe turned on a video about golf.

The girls went to their room at nine o'clock.

But they did not change into their pajamas.

Steff listened carefully. She heard Uncle Joe turn off the video.

Paulie fell asleep, still in her clothes.

Steff's eyes grew heavy.

Then, *GROAN—CREAK—CREAK—CLUNK!*

"Paulie," Steff called. "Get up."

The girls crept through the kitchen to the side door.

Mother Quigg's golf cart rolled out of the garage and down the driveway. The pink flag waved.

"Let's go!" whispered Steff.

Careful not to be seen, the girls followed the cart.

4

the pink golf cart

Mother Quigg and her golf cart soon left the houses behind. She climbed little hills and rolled around flower beds and sometimes disappeared.

"I'm tired of this." Paulie gasped for breath. "She's riding all over Lily Pad Park. We're *running* all over it."

Steff's legs felt wobbly. Paulie dropped behind.

Finally, Mother Quigg stopped.

Paulie caught up to Steff.

Steff said, "Let's go closer."

"Maybe we shouldn't. It's kind of like spying."

"It's not spying. We are *watching over* an 80-year-old woman."

"I don't think—"

"I'd say we are being helpful," Steff told her.

A harsh voice came from behind. "I'd say you are spying!"

Startled, the girls bumped into each other and tumbled to the ground.

A stranger stood above them. It looked like a man.

"Leave that woman alone," he ordered. "Get out of here."

Steff scrambled to her feet.

"Stay away from us!" she cried.

But as she stood up, she saw she was not talking to a man. She was talking to a boy only a little taller than she.

"Who are you?" she demanded. "Why did you scare us like that?"

"I don't like people spying on Mother Quigg."

Steff snapped, "You're the one who is spying."

The boy growled, "What are you doing in Lily Pad Park anyway? You don't live here."

Before Steff could answer, the pink golf cart rolled up.

Mother Quigg said, "Good evening, Cornelius. Good evening, girls." She handed each of them a daffodil. "You children hop on. I'll give you a ride home."

Steff couldn't explain to Mother Quigg why she and Paulie were there.

She didn't know why this boy named Cornelius was there.

And she certainly didn't know why Mother Quigg was there.

So Steff didn't say anything.

Neither did anyone else.

The cart whirred softly across the golf course. The only other sound was that of sprinklers coming on.

They all got a little wet.

Mother Quigg stopped the cart near the corner house.

Cornelius jumped off. He waited on the sidewalk, still holding the daffodil Mother Quigg had given him.

She drove on.

Steff remembered the night before. She remembered hearing a door close.

She whispered to Paulie, "I think Cornelius lives in the corner house. And that house is supposed to be empty."

5

giraffe in the petunias

The next morning a large box came for Mother Quigg. She opened it on the patio table.

"Girls," she said. "Just look at these packages of flower seeds. Aren't they wonderful?"

"There are so many," Steff said. "Where will you plant them?"

"Oh, here and there."

Mother Quigg put on her floppy hat. She picked two purple blossoms. She clipped them on her shoes with paper clips.

Steff read some packages. "Hollyhocks will grow much taller than marigolds. I'll make a chart that shows the heights and colors of all the plants."

Paulie told Mother Quigg, "Steff likes to organize things."

A neighbor lady called over the backyard fence. "Mother Quigg!"

A tall bush grew in front of the fence. It was trimmed to look like a giraffe.

The neighbor lady's head popped up behind the giraffe's head. "Did you hear the awful news?" she said. "I declare! We have a thief in Lily Pad Park!"

"What?" cried Mother Quigg.

Steff stopped making her chart.

The lady said, "Remember the house on the next street with the Black Pine tree in the fancy pot? I declare! That tree disappeared—fancy pot and all—right off the front porch. Stolen!"

"Terrible," said Mother Quigg.

Paulie nudged Steff. "I thought this was a safe community."

The neighbor said, "By the way, I saw

petunias near the swimming pool. The blossoms were *this* big." Her hands made a circle above the giraffe. "The grounds crew didn't know what kind of petunias they were."

"By the pool? That would be the giant ruffled petunia," said Mother Quigg.

"I declare!" said the neighbor. "I wish I knew as much about flowers as you do."

Later, Steff told Paulie, "Let's go check out the pool."

Steff made a big circle with her arms. "And we simply *must* see those giant ruffled petunias. I declare! The blossoms are *this* big. I declare!"

"You declare?" Paulie scolded her, "It's not nice to make fun of people."

Steff dropped her arms. "I know, but—"

"Your problem is you wanted to go with Mom and Dad to see your friend."

"Well, their hotel is near Amy's house. They acted like they were going to take me. Then they didn't. I haven't seen Amy since she moved away."

"It's not their fault your friend moved.

Besides, they were going to be in Amy's town only one day."

At the swimming pool, the girls found the giant ruffled petunias.

"Isn't it odd that Mother Quigg knows about these?" Steff asked. "The grounds crew didn't. I thought they planted everything."

A white wall ran behind the petunias. Bushes grew along the wall.

Steff saw something that made her cry out, "Paulie, look!" She pointed. "Where have you seen another bush like that?"

"Oh! It has been trimmed. . . . Wow!"

"Yes," said Steff. "Trimmed in the shape of a giraffe. The giraffe in the petunias is exactly like the giraffe in Mother Quigg's backyard."

"Steff, do you think Mother Quigg made this giraffe?"

"People say the Phantom Gardener made bushes into rabbits," said Steff.

"Does that mean she is the Phantom Gardener?"

"We are going to find out."

6

friend in a floppy hat

That night, long after bedtime, Mother Quigg's pink golf cart rolled down the driveway.

Steff and Paulie hurried to follow it.

The golf cart turned onto a short street and then turned again. The girls lost sight of it.

Much later, they were still looking for Mother Quigg.

They saw a large bed of roses far from any house.

Someone was dragging something to the

roses. It looked like a heavy bag. The person dropped the bag and straightened up.

Steff gasped. "It's that guy. Cornelius."

The girls crept close.

Then Steff roared in a loud, deep voice. "Cornelius! How does your garden grow?"

Cornelius whirled around. "Don't sneak up like that."

"Sneak? You're the one sneaking."

He snapped, "Do you spy on people all the time?"

Steff turned to Paulie and said, "Maybe we have found the Phantom Gardener."

"Hey!" Cornelius said. "You have it wrong. I'm not—"

Paulie laughed. "Better watch out, Cornelius. I hear Mr. Kemper is as prickly as a cactus."

"Okay, okay! I know you're teasing me," Cornelius said. "But it's nothing to joke about. This Phantom Gardener is breaking rules. The Homeowners Group could make trouble for the Phantom Gardener."

Paulie asked, "What's in the bag?"

"Plant food."

"What are you doing with it?" Steff asked.

"It's heavy. I was moving it for a friend."

"What friend?"

Just then, another person came toward them.

Cornelius pointed. "*That* friend."

The friend carried a shovel. She wore a floppy hat with a pink scarf hanging behind. White flowers glowed on the hat brim. Paulie clapped her hands to her cheeks. "Oh, no!"

Steff moaned, "It's Mother Quigg. Mother Quigg is the Phantom Gardener."

7

poppycock!

Mother Quigg said, "You girls are just in time to help feed the roses."

Paulie squeezed Steff's arm—hard.

Steff knew why. Paulie did not like being in a strange place at night—with someone called the Phantom Gardener. Even if the Phantom Gardener was a relative.

Steff didn't like it either. She said, "It's late. Let's all go home."

"Poppycock! I do my best work after the sun sets," said Mother Quigg. "Cornelius, take them to get tools from my cart."

At the golf cart, Paulie said, "We are going to get in big trouble."

Steff asked Cornelius, "So, you hang around with the Phantom Gardener?"

"I see her sometimes. We talk a little."

Paulie said, "Your parents sure let you stay out late."

"My parents don't care."

Steff said, "I know why. Your parents are away on a trip. And you're supposed to be away at school. Right, Cornelius?"

Cornelius reached into the golf cart. "Here are extra gloves. Who wants them?"

Paulie said, "We know you live in that house on the corner. You hide inside during the day. You come out at night."

"Hey," said Cornelius. "I have telephone numbers. I call my parents every day. They are busy having fun."

"Doesn't your school wonder where you are?" asked Paulie.

"Classes haven't started. If I had gone to school the day my parents left, I would have been the only kid there. So I sent the cab away. Don't worry. I'll call another cab and get to school before classes begin."

Cornelius dangled the gloves in the air. "Last chance for gloves—"

Steff said, "You are letting your parents think you are at school. You are letting them believe what is not true."

He slammed the gloves down and walked back to the roses.

Steff told Paulie, "What Cornelius is doing is wrong."

She and Paulie helped spread plant food around the roses.

A thorn stuck Steff's finger. She wished she'd worn the gloves.

At last, Mother Quigg said, "Let's pack up."

She picked a rose for each person. They hopped on the golf cart.

Mother Quigg stopped it near a bush with shiny leaves. "See that lovely camellia plant? Its blossoms look like strawberry ice cream. My heart's desire is to have a camellia plant like that. I'm saving a place in my yard for it."

Nearby grew a grove of small trees with lighted pathways.

"Oops, I nearly forgot." Mother Quigg jerked the cart to a stop. "The Mississippi magnolia tree has been doing poorly. I must take a look."

The girls and Cornelius waited in the cart.

He said, "This is called the USA grove. A tree is planted here for each state."

A cry came from the trees.

They ran to Mother Quigg.

She groaned. "Look what I've done. I stepped on the Mississippi sign. I broke it."

They picked up the pieces.

"Plastic," Mother Quigg said. "That's why it broke. I'll order a new sign made of iron."

Back in the cart, Steff asked Mother Quigg a question. She tried to ask it in a joking way. "Aren't you afraid that people will see you whizzing around in your golf cart at night?"

"Oh, pretty posies! No! All the ACTIVE seniors are at home resting for their next golf game."

"But someone might think you're the Phantom Gardener."

Mother Quigg laughed. "Phantom Gardener! Poppycock!"

a talk with
uncle joe

Early the next morning, Steff shook Paulie awake.

"Get up! We must talk to Uncle Joe before he leaves."

Uncle Joe stood in the kitchen holding a cup of coffee. "Er . . . you girls want breakfast? There must be cereal or something here."

"No, thanks," said Steff. "We'll wait."

He looked at his watch. "I have a few minutes. Let's talk."

That was exactly what Steff wanted to do.

They sat down at the table.

Uncle Joe said, "So . . . how are things?"

Steff said, "Fine."

Paulie said, "Fine."

Uncle Joe looked into his coffee cup. Then he looked at his watch again.

He said, "Great weather for golf. And other things, of course."

Steff did not want to talk about the weather. She wanted to talk about Mother Quigg being the Phantom Gardener.

She thought of a way to begin. "Lily Pad Park is beautiful. There are so many flowers."

"It's the perfect place to retire. Best golf course in this part of the country." Uncle Joe sipped his coffee.

Steff said, "Mother Quigg loves gardening."

"Yes. She doesn't play as much golf as I thought she would." He rubbed his chin. "She seems kind of tired."

They still weren't talking about the Phantom Gardener. Steff tried again. "She likes working with plants."

46

"Mother should play more golf. I've been telling the guys that my mother can beat any other woman golfer here. And she's the oldest. Of course, she can't beat anybody if she doesn't play." He looked at his watch. "Time to go."

He was leaving. Steff had to say something now!

She exclaimed, "There's a Phantom Gardener here!"

Uncle Joe chuckled. "Oh, that! Everyone at Lily Pad Park talks about a Phantom Gardener."

Steff chose her words carefully, "The Phantom Gardener seems to like gardening as much as Mother Quigg likes gardening."

"If there is a Phantom Gardener, he should spend his time golfing. That would keep him out of trouble with the Homeowners Group." Uncle Joe grinned. "I wouldn't want Mr. Kemper angry with me."

At the door, he winked. "If you girls see the Phantom Gardener, ask him to please mow the grass near the ninth hole."

The girls heard Uncle Joe's golf cart leave.

Steff told Paulie, "Uncle Joe is kind to his

mother. But he doesn't think much about what she wants. And he doesn't remember to come home for dinner."

Paulie said, "Maybe he's not honoring his mother. The Bible says *Honor your father and your mother*. That's one of the Ten Commandments God gave to Moses."

Paulie had memorized the Ten Commandments in Sunday school. She got a prize.

Steff didn't know what to do about Uncle Joe. But she did know what to do about Mother Quigg being the Phantom Gardener.

She told Paulie, "I have a plan."

9

the plan

After breakfast, the girls ran down the street.

A truck drove by. The driver was the man with the bushy eyebrows.

At the corner house, Steff knocked on the side door. She called softly, "Cornelius, it's Steff and Paulie."

The door opened a crack.

Part of the boy's face showed. "Go away."

"Wait!" Steff begged. "We want to talk about helping Mother Quigg stay out of trouble."

The door opened wider.

Cornelius stepped outside. He carried a bag of pretzels. "Follow me."

He led them to a small patio behind the garage.

"What a good hideout," Paulie exclaimed. "Nobody could see through all the bushes and potted plants around this patio."

Cornelius warned, "Shhh. Don't let the neighbors hear you. I'm supposed to be at school, remember?"

Steff sat down by a fancy pot of pansies. "I think you should tell your mom and dad you are not at school."

"You said you came to talk about helping Mother Quigg." He opened the bag of pretzels.

"Steff has a plan," Paulie told him. "Her plans work—sometimes."

"My plans work *most* times," Steff corrected her.

Steff told Cornelius, "With my plan, we can stop Mother Quigg from being the Phantom Gardener."

Cornelius sputtered, "Oh, sure we can! How?"

"Simple. We will keep her so busy during the day that she is too tired to work at night. If she can't work at night, she can't be the Phantom Gardener."

"Busy doing what?" Cornelius passed the bag of pretzels.

Steff took one. "Remember how this is a community for ACTIVE seniors? We will make Mother Quigg an ACTIVE senior."

"During the *day*," Paulie said.

"She loves gardening," said Steff. "We'll find gardening things for her to do. Our first idea is to organize a garden club. It can meet in her backyard."

Paulie reached into the pretzel bag. "The garden club can hold flower shows. People can talk about growing African violets or sunflowers."

"I just thought of something else!" Steff said. "We'll call the newspaper. They can take pictures. They can write about the plants she grows."

"Good," said Paulie. "People who read the newspaper will want to talk to her."

"Right," said Steff. "Uncle Joe will see how happy she is being a gardener. Maybe he will stop telling her to play golf."

Paulie waved a pretzel in each hand. "She's a gardener. He's a golfer. That makes a nice family. An ACTIVE family."

"A family?" Cornelius snorted. "With only two people?"

Paulie said, "Two people can be a family. Just like three people, or four people, can be a family."

Cornelius said, "Not if some of the people are always gone."

Steff snapped, "Our parents go on business trips. We're still a family."

"Steff and I get left with relatives. Some of them are . . . well, kind of different." Paulie chuckled. "Like the Phantom Gardener in the pink golf cart."

Cornelius frowned. "My parents don't travel for business. They go away because they want to. I have to live at school."

Steff glared at him. "That doesn't mean it's okay to let them believe you are in school when you're not. That's telling a lie."

Paulie said, "One of the Ten Commandments that God gave to Moses is to honor your parents. Moses told everyone that God said, *Honor your father and your mother.* It's in Exodus, chapter 20."

"Hey!" Cornelius patted his chest. "I read the Bible. Jesus talked about that commandment."

Paulie raised her eyebrows. "Well, Moses said it first. In the Old Testament."

Steff told them, "Moses and Jesus were talking about the same thing. That just shows how important it is."

They ate pretzels until the bag was empty.

Cornelius said, "More plants were stolen last night—lemon trees growing in pots."

Steff thought back to the night before. She wondered about something. She said, "Paulie and I have stuff to do—for the plan."

Out on the sidewalk, Steff told her sister, "Mother Quigg brought us home last night.

Maybe she went out again later."

"You think she moved those lemon trees?"

"She could have thought they needed more light or something."

Paulie's voice dropped to a whisper. "But if Mother Quigg took those plants, that means she is taking things away from the people who own them. That means she is more than a Phantom Gardener."

"Yes," Steff said sadly. "It means she is a thief."

No garden club?

After lunch, a telephone call came for Mother Quigg.

She hung up. "What do you know! The newspaper is coming this afternoon to take pictures of my backyard."

"You'll be famous," Paulie told her.

"Poppycock! Well, no time for a nap today. Oh, I wish I had a camellia plant. It would look nice in the pictures."

Later, Mother Quigg came to the patio. She wore a frilly dress the color of lilacs. She picked violets and tucked them behind the pink scarf on her hat.

Paulie told her, "You look beautiful."

Steff said, "That frilly dress makes me think of a tea party and pretty tea cups and you pouring tea." She nodded at Paulie.

Paulie didn't do anything.

Steff moved behind Mother Quigg and mouthed, "The plan!"

Paulie clapped her hands. "Oh! A real tea party. How fun! Mother Quigg, why don't you have an afternoon tea?"

Steff said, "Yes. People could buy tickets to come. The ticket money could buy something special for Lily Pad Park."

"Oh, pretty posies!" exclaimed Mother Quigg. "I haven't done anything like that since we moved here."

"A bench or a fountain would be a nice thing to buy," said Steff.

Mother Quigg added more violets to her hat. "Actually, I have often thought that this community needs a prayer garden."

"With a bench and a fountain," said Paulie.

"In fact," said Mother Quigg, "I know the perfect spot for a prayer garden."

"Steff and I will help." Paulie tapped her head with one finger and looked at her sister. "Now, who else will help with the tea?"

Steff answered, "I know! The Lily Pad Park Garden Club."

Mother Quigg frowned. "We don't have a garden club here."

Steff tried to sound like Mother Quigg. "No garden club? Oh, pretty posies! There should be one. You can start it."

Paulie said, "I'll get some paper. Steff and I will make a flyer about it right now."

"Yes," said Steff. "Is Monday a good day for the first meeting?"

"So soon? Well, I suppose." Mother Quigg picked more violets and began to weave them into a chain bracelet for her arm.

Steff and Paulie worked on the flyer. They stopped once to watch the newspaper person take pictures and again to talk to their parents on the phone.

When Uncle Joe came home, Steff asked if

he would make copies of the flyer.

"Garden club?" He turned to his mother. "You have seemed tired lately. Do you feel up to having a meeting here?"

"Of course. I used to do that sort of thing all the time."

Uncle Joe ate dinner with them. He went out afterward and returned at nine-thirty with the copies.

Mother Quigg and the girls sat at the kitchen table.

Uncle Joe looked surprised. "Mother, you're still up."

She asked him, "How does this sound? Cream cheese sandwiches cut in the shape of tulips."

"Tulip sandwiches? For what?"

"Why, our tea, of course. The Lily Pad Park Garden Club is holding a tea. We want to make money to build a prayer garden."

"Mother, there isn't any garden club."

"There will be."

bad news

The next morning, Paulie and Steff began putting the flyers at front doors.

Near the corner house, they heard, "Psst!"

Cornelius popped up behind a bush.

They ran to his hideout.

"Bad news!" he told them. "More plants were stolen during the night."

"How do you know?" asked Paulie.

"I saw a man come out of his house to walk his dog. He began yelling about a big fern in a basket. It was missing. Neighbors came outside.

They began to yell. Their plants were gone, too."

Steff said, "Mother Quigg went to her room last night at the same time we did."

Cornelius warned, "If the Homeowners Group learns she is the Phantom Gardener, watch out! The Phantom Gardener breaks rules. So people will think she could be doing other things—like stealing plants."

Steff had already thought of that. Worse yet—those people could be right. Maybe Mother Quigg had gone out last night, and Steff had not heard her leave.

She said, "We have to go pass out more flyers."

Cornelius showed them a yellow begonia plant in a fancy flower pot. "I'll move this near the front of the garage when I have news. It will be a signal."

Steff looked around. "You have a lot of pretty flowers and pots, Cornelius."

"If you want, you can call me Corn," he said.

Paulie said, "Corn. I like that. Do your parents call you Corn?"

"Are you kidding? Never."

"Have you asked them to?"

"Sort of."

As the girls passed out flyers, Steff told Paulie, "I don't think Corn can talk to his parents very well."

Near the Quiggs' house, they saw the man with the bushy eyebrows. He walked across the street carrying clippers.

Steff said, "I wonder if that man is looking for the grounds crew. He is always by himself."

That afternoon, Mother Quigg made many telephone calls. She did not take a nap.

That night, she stayed up late looking for pictures of benches and fountains.

The next morning, Mother Quigg had another idea. "The garden club can grow seedlings and give them away."

Each day, the girls tried to keep Mother Quigg busy.

Each night, Steff stayed awake as long as she

could. She listened for the sound of the pink golf cart.

On Monday, the Lily Pad Park Garden Club held its first meeting.

Most of the talk was about stolen plants.

The garden club chose Mother Quigg as its president.

The next day, a small, heavy package came for Mother Quigg.

It lay on the kitchen table where Steff was writing a list of garden club plans. She moved the package out of her way.

Paulie ran in. She was out of breath. "The yellow begonia is by Corn's garage."

Steff said, "That's the signal! Let's go."

12

ſecret patrol

They found Cornelius in his hideout.

He told them, "Last night, I was near the clubhouse. Some people from the Homeowners Group came outside and talked. Wow! They *really* want to catch the thief. A few people will walk through the community every night and keep watch. No one else will know."

"A secret patrol," said Steff.

"And that's not all. The patrol begins to-night! Exciting, huh?" said Cornelius. "When my parents hear about it, they will wish they had not gone away."

The girls walked back to Uncle Joe's house.

Steff said, "Something bothers me. Corn acts almost as if he likes plants being stolen. Maybe he thinks his parents will stay home more if exciting things happen at Lily Pad Park."

"Oh, Steff! Corn couldn't be a thief."

"There are a lot of nice potted plants in his hideout. And he goes everywhere after dark," Steff said. "Somebody is stealing plants."

"It can't be Corn," said Paulie. "It can't be Mother Quigg, either."

"I hope not. But who is it?"

That night, everyone at the Quigg house went to bed at ten o'clock.

Later, something woke Steff.

GROAN—CREAK—CREAK—CLUNK!

The garage door was opening.

Steff ran to the window.

The pink golf cart rolled down the driveway, its pink flag waving.

"Paulie," Steff called. "Mother Quigg just drove away."

Paulie sat up. "The Homeowners patrol will see her."

"We have to stop her."

The girls dressed and dashed toward the side door.

But Steff ran back and pounded on Uncle Joe's bedroom door.

"Uncle Joe!" she cried. "Mother Quigg drove away in her golf cart. We are going to find her. Can you help?"

Sleepy noises came from inside the bedroom. "What did you say? Golf cart?"

Steff yelled, "Your mother is the Phantom Gardener."

"You're having a dream. Go back to bed."

"It's not a dream. Mother Quigg is about to get caught by the Homeowners patrol."

The girls rushed out of the house.

Someone came running up.

Steff's stomach did a giant flip-flop. "Corn! Don't scare us like that."

"I was coming to tell you I saw Mother Quigg driving down the street."

The girls and Cornelius raced past one corner and then another. They did not see the pink golf cart.

Finally, they dropped to the ground out of breath.

Steff said, "Let's organize this search. Let's think. Where was she the last night we were with her?"

Paulie remembered. "Putting plant food on the roses."

"And she showed us her heart's desire," said Steff. "The camellia plant with blossoms the color of strawberry ice cream."

"We stopped in the USA grove to check on the Mississippi magnolia tree," said Cornelius.

"Yes. She broke the sign. She said she'd order a new one."

"One made of iron. She doesn't like plastic signs," said Cornelius.

Steff remembered something. "A small package came this morning. A heavy package. It must have been the iron sign. That's it! Mother Quigg is taking the sign to the USA grove."

Cornelius started to get up. At once, he dropped back to the ground. "Shhh!"

Two people walked toward them.

13

MOTHER QUIGG'S
HEART'S DESIRE

The girls huddled close to a hibiscus bush.

Cornelius peeked over the bush. He whispered, "It's Mr. Kemper and another man."

The men stopped and talked.

Steff and the others waited.

Steff felt terrible. It was awful to think that either Mother Quigg or Cornelius might be taking people's plants. She prayed neither one was the thief.

Cornelius tore a leaf into tiny pieces. "I've been thinking. . . ."

"What?" asked Steff.

He kept watching Mr. Kemper. "About what Moses and Jesus said. That God told us to honor our parents."

He pointed. "Two more people just walked up. Now they're all talking."

Steff reminded him, "You were saying something about honoring your parents."

"Yes. Well, I decided that I was not doing that—honoring them, I mean. So I called them tonight and told them where I was."

Steff said, "I'm glad, Corn."

Paulie asked, "Were they very angry?"

Cornelius said, "At first. Then I told them the honor part. Mom started crying. And I told them the part about being a family of three."

"An ACTIVE family of three," said Paulie.

"Anyway, they are coming home *tomorrow*! I can't believe they're coming home early from a trip!"

Steff swallowed a lump in her throat. "That's good, Corn, really good."

Cornelius smiled. "I know."

He stood up. "Those people left. We can go now."

Cornelius and the girls hurried toward the USA Grove. They crossed a narrow dirt road with few streetlights.

Steff said, "A truck is parked down that road where it's dark."

"Probably belongs to the grounds crew," said Cornelius. "That land is part of the community, but houses haven't been built on it yet."

They came to where Mother Quigg had shown them her heart's desire—the camellia plant.

Steff stopped. Something was wrong. Terribly wrong.

Paulie cried, "The camellia plant! It's gone."

In its place, they found a dark hole in the ground.

Steff felt as if she had fallen into a dark hole.

Cornelius said, "Mother Quigg must have wanted that camellia plant so much that she dug it up and took it."

Paulie wailed, "That means that Mother Quigg . . ."

"What was she thinking?" Steff moaned. "People will see the camellia in her backyard. Is she going to tell everyone she bought it at a store?"

Cornelius said, "The Homeowners patrol could come any second. We must find Mother Quigg. The USA grove is this way. Come on."

They had barely started when Steff shouted, "Look! Here is the camellia."

It lay on its side on the ground near some big bushes. Other plants in pots lay nearby.

Paulie gasped. "Those potted plants belong to people."

Cornelius said, "All this stuff is stolen."

At least Steff knew now that Cornelius had not taken the plants. If he had, he would not have brought her and Paulie to where he had hidden them. But she looked at the camellia and moaned, "Oh no, Mother Quigg must have stolen all of it."

Footsteps sounded on the street.

"The Homeowners patrol!" Cornelius put a

finger to his lips. "If they catch us here, they will think *we* are stealing the plants."

Paulie whispered, "Should we run?"

Cornelius nodded. "We have to. Right now!"

Steff grabbed Paulie's hand.

They followed Cornelius for a few steps.

"Wait!" Steff hissed. "We can't run away. I know it seems as if Mother Quigg is a thief. But could there be a mistake?"

"I wish. . . ." said Cornelius.

"What can we do?" Paulie squealed.

Steff said, "We need to talk to Mother Quigg. And we need to get these pots back to the owners. Let's hide them in the bushes for now. Tomorrow we'll try to move them to where the owners will find them."

"Okay," said Cornelius. "Hurry! I'll put the camellia back in the ground."

Steff told Paulie, "Quick, help me drag the pots out of sight."

They moved all the pots except one. It held a small tree.

The girls bent down and grabbed the

branches. They pulled, inching toward the bushes, dragging the heavy pot.

Back, back they went.

Suddenly, a man stepped out of the shadows.

14

imagine that!

THUMP! The man tripped over the small tree.

He sprawled on the ground near Steff's feet. "Ooof!"

The girls dropped the tree and screamed.

The man hollered, "What's going on?"

Cornelius yelled, "Steff, Paulie! Run!"

The man raised up on his knees. Even in the dark, Steff saw his bushy eyebrows.

The girls dashed toward Cornelius.

Steff looked back.

The man pointed at them. He was getting to his feet.

Just then, someone jumped from the bushes.

A shovel flashed through the air.

WHACK!

"Y-E-O-W!" The man toppled to the ground and lay there groaning.

Mother Quigg stood over him, holding her shovel.

People ran up. One was a guard from the gate. Two men grabbed the man on the ground.

Mr. Kemper said, "Mother Quigg, you got the thief we have been looking for."

Mother Quigg put her shovel down. "Good evening, Mr. Kemper. How nice that you came along."

The guard said, "This thief has been stealing plants from homes in the community. He took these tonight and was carrying them to his truck."

Cornelius asked, "The truck parked on the dirt road?"

"Yes," said Mr. Kemper. "It looks like the

ones used by our grounds crew. At night, he would put stolen plants in his truck and hide it. In the daytime, he would drive it out of the park and unload the stolen plants. Then he would drive the truck back in."

The guard said, "We let him through the gate because we thought he worked with the grounds crew. Instead, he was stealing plants to sell."

Just then a golf cart zoomed up.

Uncle Joe jumped out. He wore pajamas and waved a golf club. "I've been trying to find you. Is everyone all right?" He hugged Mother Quigg. He hugged the girls. He even hugged Cornelius.

"Uncle Joe," cried Paulie. "Mother Quigg hit a bad man with her shovel."

Uncle Joe turned to his mother. "Mother?" His voice cracked.

Mr. Kemper said, "This thief had us fooled. People kept saying Lily Pad Park had a Phantom Gardener. They said the Phantom Gardener helped make our community beautiful. But lately, everyone began to believe the

Phantom Gardener was stealing plants."

Uncle Joe cleared his throat. He looked at Mother Quigg. "A Phantom Gardener. Imagine that."

Mr. Kemper looked at Mother Quigg. "Imagine that."

Mother Quigg said, "Imagine that."

She touched her hat. A giant ruffled petunia blossom fluttered to the ground.

Mother Quigg said, "I've done a bit of gardening here and a bit of gardening there. I never met a Phantom Gardener."

Steff moved over and stood on the petunia.

Mr. Kemper told Mother Quigg, "I understand you are the president of a new garden club. The Homeowners Group wants the garden club to have the job of making sure Lily Pad Park stays beautiful."

She said, "I'm sure the club will be happy to do that."

"Good," said Mr. Kemper. "Of course, there would never, never be any *night* work."

"Of course." Another giant ruffled petunia fluttered from Mother Quigg's hat.

Mr. Kemper said good-bye and walked away.

Mother Quigg told Uncle Joe, "This means I won't have time to play golf."

Uncle Joe said, "I understand. Actually, I understand a *lot* of things." He put his arm around his mother. "From now on, you can be the gardener in the family—or whatever you want. I'll be the golfer. But let's save some time to do things together."

Paulie poked Cornelius. "See, I told you they could be an ACTIVE family of two."

Steff grinned at Mother Quigg and Uncle Joe. "Thanks for letting us stay with you. It's fun here."

Uncle Joe said, "If you girls had not come, the rumor of the Phantom Gardener at Lily Pad Park might have hung around a long time."

He took Mother Quigg's shovel. He put it on one shoulder and his golf club on the other. "Let's go home."

Mother Quigg said, "First, I must finish putting a sign by the Mississippi tree. Want to help?"

Steff and Paulie walked behind the others.

Steff thought about Cornelius. At first he had not honored his parents. He had not told them the truth.

Maybe Uncle Joe had not honored his mother. He was good to her. He gave her a pink golf cart. But he didn't listen to what she wanted to do.

Steff thought about herself and her parents.

She said, "Paulie, I have been feeling sorry for myself."

Paulie groaned. "No kidding!"

"Well, I'm stopping that. Mom and Dad are great. We have a great family."

"We sure do." Paulie giggled. "We have a great, ACTIVE family of four."

Steff laughed. "More—if you count all our relatives. I should make a list."

the end